ELLIOTT

ELLIOTT

by Peggy Clifford

drawings by Jacqueline Chwast

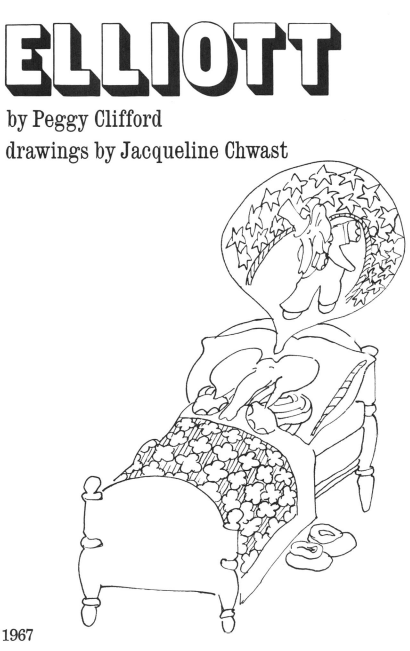

1967

HOUGHTON MIFFLIN COMPANY BOSTON

Once upon a time, there was a six-year-old girl named Juliana who asked me to tell her a bedtime story. This is it . . . and it is dedicated to her with much love.

ELLIOTT

$\bigcirc$NCE UPON a time there was a young elephant named Elliott. He was a perfectly ordinary elephant — except for one thing. Elliott was very, very small. Since the idea of elephant is BIG, Elliott was almost constantly embarrassed by his lack of size.

He had a pitifully short trunk and no tusks at all, so he could not carry the immense

burdens that elephants are supposed to be able to carry. His friends could pick up large logs. Exerting all his strength and willpower, Elliott could pick up one very small log. Elephants are also supposed to be able to use their trunks like hoses. But when Elliott and his friends were sporting about in the stream near the village, Elliott was always last in the squirting contests. His friends could spray the tops of tall trees. Elliott, after huffing and puffing with all of his might, could only manage a sad, little dribble. And elephants are supposed to have great stamina, to travel long distances and do hard work without tiring. Elliott, because of his size, always had trouble keeping up and tired easily in pulling contests. In fact, Elliott was rather a joke among the other elephants.

But, despite his handicaps, Elliott had a lot of spirit. He was not discouraged by the jokes about his short trunk. He thought to himself: "A long trunk isn't everything. Monkeys and tigers don't have any trunks at all and they seem happy enough. Why, the king of beasts, the lion, doesn't even have a trunk. Trunks, after all, are highly overrated." If almost everybody in the world could get along without a trunk, then surely Elliott shouldn't put too much emphasis on his. In fact, an elephant who was not dependent on his trunk might actually be considered a superior sort of beast.

Elliott decided one day when the sun was high and the shadows in the grass were short that he would train himself in other directions. He already knew how to play chess. But you couldn't play chess by yourself and all the other elephants thought it was a terrible bore. Besides, when they lost, they got very angry and swept the chessmen off the board with their trunks.

No, Elliott thought, he must do something distinctly athletic. Something that none of the other elephants could do. Elliott had

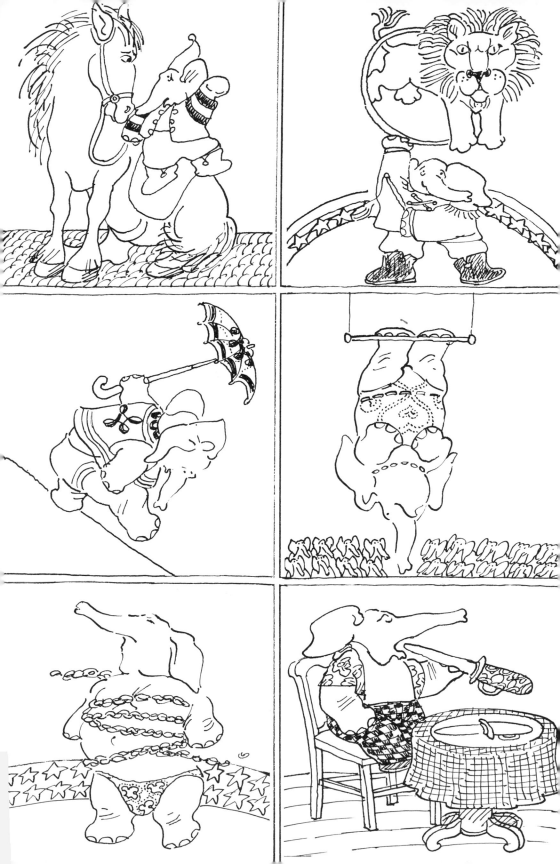

always been fascinated by the circus, so perhaps he might do something circusy. He eliminated the tight rope right away, because heights made him a little bit nervous. For that reason, he had always been glad he wasn't a monkey, since they spent most of their time in the tops of tall trees. He would enjoy doing tricks on the back of a horse, but he didn't know any horses who would want even a small, friendly elephant clomping around on their backs. He considered a lion act, but none of the lions in his neighborhood took him very seriously so he wasn't sure how they'd feel about his cracking whips at them.

For several days, Elliott wandered about in a cloud of thoughts. He thought of and discarded trapezes (height again), sword-swallowing (sounded awfully unpleasant), getting out of trunks (too confining), breaking chains with his chest (didn't seem likely that he could do it) and countless other circus acts. But finally one day, feeling very discouraged, he was sitting under a tree, chewing on a daisy, when it came to him. He knew in a flash what his feat would be. He, Elliott, the smallest elephant of all, would do a somersault on a trampoline! Oh, it was a lovely idea.

He closed his eyes and pictured himself looping slowly through the air and landing gracefully on his feet, with a small, proud smile on his face, bowing to his audience. Well, it would take some doing, but he felt full of confidence and he WOULD do it. Of course, he would have to have a trampoline and, as he was rather short of cash, he decided to make one.

Before he made any plans, he would visit Sir Augustus, an old elephant who had been in the circus for years and recently retired with full honors. Sir Augustus could tell him all about trampolines. Elliott would arrange to see him tomorrow. One couldn't simply drop in on Sir Augustus, because he was a very important elephant with a very stern

7

and serious expression on his face and lots of dignity. An impressive figure of an elephant . . . quite dashing, in an elderly way. Actually, he resembled a British Army officer.

The next morning, after a quick breakfast of grapes and ivy leaves, Elliott set out for the house of Sir Augustus. It was a lovely day and darts of sun danced on the flowers. It looked like a very lucky day. When he got to Sir Augustus's house, he knocked politely on the door. There was no answer. Everyone knew that Sir Augustus was a little deaf, but no one talked about it. Finally, Elliott grew bold and hammered with all his might. From deep inside the house boomed a voice:

"Who's that knocking at my door?"

"It's me, Sir. Elliott, the smallest elephant of all. I would like to make an appointment to see you." Elliott didn't see why, since they were both there, with nothing better to do, they couldn't talk right now. But that wasn't the way Sir Augustus did things.

8

"Let's see," boomed the voice, "let me look at my appointment pad. Ah. How about a week from tomorrow at 2:30 P.M.?"

"Well, Sir," Elliott cleared his throat and began again, "Well, Sir, it's rather urgent. Could we make it today?"

"Today! Today! That's awfully short notice for an appointment. Well, I suppose if it's urgent . . . you say it's urgent?"

"Yes, Sir. It's very urgent."

"Well, then, in that case. Let's see. How about 10 A.M.? I could squeeze you in for a few minutes then. But only for a few minutes, you understand. I'm a very busy elephant. Lots on my mind. Lots to do."

Elliott knew that Sir Augustus spent most of his time cheating at solitaire, but he said: "Yes, Sir. I know, Sir. I would certainly appreciate a few moments of your time, Sir."

"All right, young elephant. Come back at 10 A.M. But be punctual. I detest tardiness. And I have a lot on my mind."

"Yes, Sir. I'll be here promptly. And thank you, Sir."

There was no answer from inside, so Elliott wandered down the path. He thought of picking some flowers for Sir Augustus, but he decided that the majestic old codger probably thought flowers were frivolous. So he went home and drew some designs for a trampoline.

He would use logs for the frame. Mahogany logs would look best, he thought. He was puzzled over what to use for the actual mat. Woven straw would look rather snappy, but he wasn't sure — even though he was the smallest elephant of all — that it would hold him up.

Sir Augustus would probably have lots of good ideas about making a trampoline . . . even in the middle of the forest, because Sir was an EXPERT. Elliott wasn't sure what an EXPERT was, but he did know that EXPERTS seemed to know more than he did. He had never met one . . . except Sir Augustus

. . . but he had read a lot of books by experts. He knew that they were written by EXPERTS because it usually said in the front of the book: "This book was written by an expert."

Drawing himself up to his full height, which was, we must confess, under four feet, Elliott rapped smartly on Sir's door at precisely 10 A.M. He heard nothing so he knocked again and suddenly the door flew away from under his knuckles and he practically fell down at a very stern Sir Augustus's feet.

"WHAT! What? What's all the commotion about? Who is it? Speak up! Speak up!" Sir Augustus was glowering darkly and flailing his trunk about so impatiently that his gold-rimmed glasses nearly fell off.

"It's me, Sir. Elliott. We have an appointment."

Augustus looked down. "Oh. Oh, yes. Well, come in, come in. But be quick about it. I have lots to do. A lot on my mind. Lots to do."

Timidly, Elliott went into the house. It was an awesome place, filled with fading circus posters, featuring Sir Augustus, of course, and trophies and dusty old feather plumes. There was very little in the room which didn't have to do — in one way or another — with circuses. Elliott thought to himself that Sir Augustus was a very single-minded elephant. Elliott decided that he would be VERY single-minded about his feats on the trampoline.

Looking very business-like, Sir Augustus cleared his throat and said, "Well, my boy, don't just stand there gaping. Let's get on with it. What DO you want? I'm very busy. Lots on my mind."

Elliott looked at the floor and hiccuped once and said, "You see, Sir, I'm a very small elephant..."

"Yes, unfortunate. Anyone can see that. No need, my boy, to point that out. Never point out the obvious. Bores people."

"Well, I'm very small and no one in the village takes me very seriously."

"Can't blame them for that, lad. Hard to take a tiny elephant seriously. After all, the very idea of ELEPHANT means something BIG. Think of elephant, my boy, and you think of BIG."

"Well, I thought if I could do something that none of the other elephants can do . . . well, I thought, they might take me more seriously. I mean, then they'd admire me and I'd like that . . ." Elliott's voice trailed off. He was losing confidence in his plan. It sounded silly and rather vain, too.

"Yes, yes. Sound thinking . . . though why you'd care about having the esteem of a bunch of backwoods elephants like these, I can't imagine. Such boors. Not a wit among them. And no style. Utterly ridiculous group. Never traveled. Don't want to. Oh, the things I've put up with since I retired! That's why I seldom go out. Too boring."

14

Elliott took heart. He beamed. If Sir Augustus, the smartest, wisest elephant of all, thought that his idea was good, it must be very good indeed. Brilliant perhaps.

"Just what is it, lad, that you're going to do to impress these clods? Take something terrific, you know. Something unusual. Maybe even spectacular."

"Well, Sir, I thought I might learn to do a flip on a trampoline. It's something elephants don't ordinarily do. I mean . . . being so big and all."

Sir Augustus's normal bored expression vanished. He was plainly astonished. His eyes grew very wide . . . well, as wide as an elephant's eyes can get which, to tell you the truth, isn't very wide. Despite their great size, elephants have very small eyes. "My boy! A FLIP ON A TRAMPOLINE! My boy! What a singular idea! Astounding! An elephant doing a flip. Why you'll be the toast of the forest! A hero!" He paused, lit

15

a cigar, inhaled and blew several vague smoke rings. "But it can't be done, lad. Can't be done!"

Tears welled up in Elliott's eyes. And in a very small voice he said, "Why not, Sir Augustus? Why not?"

"Well, lad, no need to weep. Face up to the impossible, that's my motto. When you see something's impossible, drop it. Forget it. Go on to something else."

"But why *can't* I do a flip on a trampoline?" Elliott felt overwhelmingly sad.

"Well, my boy, I never heard of an elephant doing one and you're hardly big enough to try something none of our noble forebears has ever done. Hardly big enough at all, my boy. I mean, firsts are tasks for full-sized elephants."

"But that's just it, Sir Augustus! A big elephant couldn't do it . . . because he'd be too big. He'd get in his own way."

"My dear boy," Sir Augustus drew himself

16

up to his full height, "have you ever seen anyone do a flip on a trampoline?" He looked very stern.

"Well, no. I've never actually been to a circus. But I've read about it." Elliott made a circle on the rug with his toe.

"Well, there you are. You don't even know what it is you're going to do. Reading is no substitute for experience. I didn't learn what I know by reading. I learned by experience. Experience is the great teacher, lad."

Elliott wished Sir Augustus weren't quite so fond of the sound of his own voice. "Well, Sir. Yes, Sir. That's why I came to you. I thought you could tell me about it from your experience."

"Well, I'll be glad to, my boy. Glad to. But it won't do you much good. Because you can't do it. Listen, the people who do flips on trampolines are very small and slim and trim and graceful. Why, they're like monkeys. Monkeys would be very good on trampolines if they weren't so silly. Monkeys don't like to work, to train. They just like to swing about in the trees. Silly, frivolous creatures. Nothing on THEIR minds but jokes and bananas. Well, anyway, these acrobats are very light on their feet. Elephants have many fine qualities, but agility isn't one, my boy. No, you should concentrate on feats of strength, not acrobatics. Simply not our line of work, boy."

"But, Sir, I'm so small. I'm not like other elephants." He had an inspiration. "If I show you that I'm graceful, will you help me?"

"Let me think. Hmmmm. Very unusual request. Yes. Hurrumph. Hmmm. Never undertaken anything quite like this before. Oh, I've been associated with acrobats before. Very nice class of people. Trim. Hardworking. But I've never actually HELPED one — especially one as short and square as you. No offense, my boy. No offense. But you certainly are a most unusual acrobat. Well, let's see what you can do."

"Do you have a rope, Sir?"

"A rope? A rope! Well, I have a clothesline. Would that do?"

"That'll be fine. May I get it? Where is it?"

"Out in back." Sir was very curious and couldn't imagine what Elliott was going to do with his clothesline. But Sir seldom asked questions. He didn't feel it was dignified. So he merely lit another cigar and blew some very dignified smoke-rings . . . and gazed at the ceiling.

Elliott was back in a moment with the clothesline which was about twenty feet long. "Sir Augustus, I don't suppose you'd like me to cut this, would you? I mean, it's probably twenty feet long because you want it to be twenty feet long."

Sir Augustus snorted. No one would catch HIM treasuring so mundane a thing as a clothesline. Besides, he could always tie the pieces together again and it would be good as new. He gestured grandly and said:

19

"Cut it, my boy. Cut it. Dice it, if you wish."

Elliott took out his Boy Scout knife. Actually, he wasn't a Boy Scout. The others thought he was too little. But he had sent away for the knife. "I'll just cut off a short piece here. About six feet." And so he did.

"Now, Sir Augustus, I will show you that I am graceful."

And to Sir Augustus's profound astonishment and amazement, Elliott began jumping rope! Slowly, ponderously, but he WAS jumping rope. "My boy! Where did you learn to do THAT? Why, it's astonishing! Amazing! Why, it's incredible! There's your trick, boy! There's your trick. You don't need the trampoline. Stick to rope-jumping, boy, and you'll see your name in lights."

Now Elliott was crossing the ends of the rope back and forth gracefully in front of him and jumping along, humming quietly to himself: "1-2-3 . . . 1-2-3." Now he was hopping on one foot. Now bouncing on two. Finally, he stopped. He had not missed once.

"You see, Sir Augustus. I AM graceful." Elliott couldn't help smiling as he said it. He had never done so well with the jump rope.

"My boy, it's true! You ARE graceful. But I don't understand why this isn't enough for you. Why must you go on to the trampoline? Why not stick to jump-roping? You are a wizard at it. A wizard!"

"Well, my Cousin Edward who lives in another part of the forest taught me to do this. He's quite a bit older than I am, but he's very small, too. I think smallness runs in my family. Anyway, Edward is much better than I am. He can do all sorts of tricks that I can't do. You see, it's HIS stunt. And I want a stunt all my own. That's why I've chosen the trampoline. That will be MY stunt."

Sir Augustus understood. He himself had never reached the pinnacle of success because

lots of elephants could do the things he did. For all his dignity and pomp and posing, he really had been a very run-of-the-mill circus elephant. Not that he'd admit it to anyone. It was foolish to talk about one's inadequacies. After all, what was the point? But, in any case, he understood what Elliott was talking about. He would help the spunky young elephant and perhaps he might even become his manager . . . "Sir Augustus proudly presents Elliott The Elephant and His Trampoline." He could see it now . . . in lights. A whole new career. An impresario.

"Yes, indeed, Elliott, I understand. I will help you. Let's get started right now. Immediately. No point in lolling about. There's lots to be done. Let's get at it. What's first, boy? What's first?"

Elliott was very excited that this great old elephant was going to help him. He felt like leaping about and shouting, but he knew that that wouldn't do at all. One must, after all, maintain a certain amount of decorum and dignity at all times around Sir Augustus. Because he was, after all, an eminence.

"Well, Sir, first, we have to make a trampoline."

"Good logic, boy. Good logic." He chuckled. "Yes, indeed. We can't do much without one, can we? Can hardly get on with our project at all without a trampoline. Now, first things first! Where shall we build it? We'll need a big clearing so that when you're ready for an audience, there'll be room for one. On the other hand, we want some sort of out-of-the-way place, so we can keep your stunt a secret. You know, boy, the less people know about what you're doing the better. That's always been a rule of mine."

"Yes, Sir. Well, there's a perfect spot up on the cliff. None of the other elephants go up there because it's such a steep climb. But there's a big clearing."

"Steep climb, eh?" Sir looked dubious.

"Well, we must make sacrifices. And my wind is as good as it ever was. You're sure it's private though? We'll need plenty of privacy. We don't want anyone horning in on our act."

Elliott tried not to smile. Sir Augustus was already calling it "our" act when only five minutes ago, he'd been completely against it. But he would be a great help. And he'd be a grand announcer for the act. Why, it would really be just like the circus with Sir Augustus helping. They might even serve pink lemonade to make it an OCCASION.

"Now! We've decided that. What's next, boy?"

"Well, we have to decide what to make the trampoline out of."

"Yes, Hmm. It's one decision after another this morning, my boy. Well, let me think . . ." Augustus lit another cigar. "Too bad you're too young for cigars, boy. They're a great help when you're making decisions."

"Well, Sir. I have a few ideas." Elliott

spoke timidly, because he knew that if he wanted Augustus's help, he had better let him make most of the decisions. Old elephants always make the important decisions. That's one of the first rules of the forest.

Augustus looked vaguely annoyed. "Yes, boy. Well, speak up. Speak up."

"Well, I thought we might make the frame of mahogany. It's hard and really quite nice-looking, too."

"Capital idea, my boy. Simply capital."

Elliott didn't know what that meant, but he hoped it was good. He went on, "But I don't know what to make the mat from."

"Hmmmmm. What will we make the mat out of? Any ideas?"

Elliott was disappointed. He had hoped that Sir would have lots of ideas about the mat, for he hadn't any. "No, Sir," he said. "I had hoped that you would be able to think of something. I would bounce right through any sort of woven straw and crash to the ground.

It would be very embarrassing. But I can't think of anything else."

"Well, let's see. Banana tree leaves would look nice, but I doubt that you could get much bounce out of them. Palm fronds would be very ticklish and not terribly substantial either. Let me think." Sir Augustus struck a thoughtful pose.

Elliott stood very, very still so as not to disturb Sir and held his breath. If hopes were horses, a herd would have been galloping through Elliott's head. Surely someone as worldly and sophisticated as Sir Augustus would be able to think of the perfect trampoline mat.

At that moment, Sir Augustus shouted: "I've got it!"

"You do? What is it? Oh, tell me or I'll burst from excitement! Please, Sir, what is it?"

"Well, stop prattling and I'll tell you." He raised his trunk and waved it around majestically. "Now listen."

27

Elliott could see plainly that Sir enjoyed a little drama and suspense. "Please, Sir. Please do go on!"

"All right. All right. Patience, my boy. Patience! Now listen carefully." He paused. "We'll borrow a piece of canvas from the game warden's tent!"

Elliott was astonished. "WE'LL BORROW a piece of canvas from the game warden's tent?"

"Yes, my boy. It IS a good idea if I do say so myself."

"Well, Sir, I mean . . ." Elliott paused and took a deep breath. "I mean, how can we BORROW a piece of someone's tent? I don't mean to be disrespectful, Sir, but it's a bit like BORROWING a match. Even if you give it back, it's not worth much."

"OH! Yes . . . well, I hadn't thought of it that way. Never really liked the game warden very much anyway. Awfully pompous fellow. Thought it might be a good trick if he woke up one morning and found a big hole in his tent. Funny picture, if I do say so myself." And he snapped his suspenders for emphasis.

"SIR!"

"What, boy? No need to shout like that. Startles one. I'm right here. Right here, boy. Now what is it?"

"Well, Sir, your suspenders . . ."

"What about them, boy? What about them? Perfectly ordinary. I've had them for years. Only I call them braces . . . sounds more dignified somehow."

"Well, Sir, your . . . er . . . braces. If we collected a lot of suspenders we could make a perfect trampoline mat! Oh my, it would be terribly bouncy. Why I could bounce to the tree tops and down again. I could do TWO flips in the air. I could . . ."

"Calm down, boy. Calm down. Let me think." Sir thought it was an awfully good idea, but he didn't want to seem too excited. It wasn't dignified, for one thing. For another, it might make Elliott conceited, and conceit wasn't attractive in very young elephants. Invariably, older elephants had pride, while younger elephants had ordinary conceit. Age mellows all things, Augustus thought. "Yes, my boy, I think it MIGHT work. Might work. If, of course, we can find enough suspenders. And IF their owners will be willing to part with them. I, of course, will be happy to donate mine to such a worthy cause."

Elliott wished that Sir Augustus wouldn't always be so grand about everything, but he smiled and said: "Oh, thank you, Sir. Thank you very much. I'm sure that once the other elephants know that you have made such a generous gesture, they will want to follow your fine example. How many do you suppose we'll need?"

"Well, my boy, let's see. Let's sit down and figure it out logically." He plomped down heavily at the table and reached for paper and pencil. "Have a chair, boy. Sit down."

Elliott sat down. "Well, Sir, I think it'll have to be about nine feet by five feet. Each suspender is about an inch wide and there are twelve inches in a foot and nine times twelve is . . ." He frowned and squinted and concentrated as hard as he could. "Sir, what IS nine times twelve?"

"Just a minute, boy. Just a minute. I'm a circus elephant not a mathematician." Sir was busily writing numbers on a piece of paper. "Let's see. Yes. Nine times twelve is . . . ah . . . it's 1008."

"No, Sir! That CAN'T be right!"

"Hmmm. No, boy. No, it certainly doesn't look right. Let's try it again." He scribbled some more. "Hmm. Yes. And carry the one. Oh, yes! Yes, got one too many zeroes in there. Yes. It's 108. And if each suspender strap is one inch wide. Then one pair is two inches wide. So we'll need . . ." Sir scribbled some more. "Yes, two into 108 go, let's see. Five

31

and four. Fifty-four! We'll need fifty-four pairs of suspenders going across. And then we probably should have some going lengthwise. We can clip two pairs together to make them long enough. Probably should have four sets of two. That's eight more. And eight and fifty-four are . . ." He did some more figuring on his paper. "YES! Why, sixty-two, of course."

Elliott's head was reeling from all these numbers. He was certainly glad that Sir was so good at arithmetic.

"Sixty-two pairs! That's a lot, boy. Well, we have mine. So we only need to find sixty-one more pairs. Somehow sixty-one seems a lot less formidable than sixty-two. Doesn't it?"

Elliott thought that must be an older elephant's kind of logic, because it didn't seem less to him. Older elephants were really QUITE different from younger elephants.

"But, Sir, how can we get all the suspenders

we need without someone's suspecting that we're up to something? I had planned the whole stunt as a surprise. But there's certainly nothing normal about an elephant's going about and collecting *61* pairs of suspenders. I mean, what will they think? If I have to tell everyone I borrow suspenders from what I'm going to do, then everyone in the jungle will soon know what I'm up to."

"Yes. That's definitely a problem. Let me see. We could tell them that you wanted to make a slingshot to shoot grapes out of the trees."

"Begging your pardon, Sir, but then 61 elephants would be expecting to see me shooting at grapes. I'm afraid that I'd soon begin to feel quite self-conscious. Let's see . . . what can we say?" Elliott frowned. "I know! I have it! I could make 61 belts out of grape vines and offer to trade them for the suspenders. I could explain that belts are more MODERN than suspenders. Most elephants like the idea of being modern, so they would all think that I was doing them a favor."

"Most elephants like being modern? Indeed! I have always thought that most elephants were silly creatures and this proves it. To want to be modern just for the sake of being modern indicates a very frivolous nature. Tradition, my boy. Tradition is what matters."

Elliott didn't feel it was the time to get into an argument, so he said: "Yes, Sir. But do you think the idea will work?"

Sir sighed: "I suppose so. Unfortunate . . . but I suppose it will. Too bad that elephants care so little about tradition. I mean, they have terribly long memories. So they remember the good old things. They just don't care about them. My boy, elephants have a noble history. I assume you've heard of Hannibal? Well, my boy, it was elephants who gave Hannibal his victory."

Elliott knew that if Augustus started reminiscing, they'd waste half the day. "I know, Sir, we studied it in school. It was a glorious victory for elephants. But I think we'd better start collecting the vines for the belts."

Elliott spent the better part of a week collecting vines while Sir Augustus shouted at him. Every morning they'd go out together. Sir Augustus was so captivated by his new role as impresario that he'd canceled all of his appointments and given up solitaire. He was a star-maker now, and he sat like a star-maker under an umbrella of banana tree leaves and shouted at Elliott who was cutting the vines with a bread knife and a very ornate, very squeaky pair of scissors. Sometimes he shouted: "NO! NO! Not that one, my boy. That's much too thick." Other times, he intoned: "NO! STOP, my boy. Too thin, too thin!" In fact, Elliott wasn't even thinking of that one, he'd just brushed past it on his way to some nice, supple vines which would be good for weaving into belts.

But he never complained, because, as far as he knew, he was the only elephant in the whole forest with a manager. He had read someplace that you don't have a manager unless you are a real success. Occasionally, when he was hot and tired, he thought he might just settle for having a manager. After all, none of his friends had managers. He could just strut about and say grandly, to the bigger elephants, "Well, I have a manager." But it wasn't a very satisfying thought. Elliott didn't really want to boast, he simply wanted to show the bigger elephants that HE had an accomplishment, that even if he was very small, he was able to do SOMETHING. So Sir Augustus kept shouting and Elliott kept cutting vines.

Finally, Sir's storeroom was filled to the roof with vines. Now neither Sir Augustus nor Elliott had ever woven a belt before . . .

or anything else for that matter. In general, elephants are not apt to be weavers. Close work usually makes an elephant's eyes smart. On the other hand, elephants are very persistent and so finally — after a lot of talk — they braided 61 very striking belts.

The belts varied in length and width, because elephants vary in length and width. But most of them were a very attractive greenish color, shot with a little brown. They had surprising snap and stretch and Elliott was confident that he and his noisy manager would be able to fit nearly every elephant in the forest. The belts fastened with an ingenious little loop and a button made of an acorn.

When Elliott surveyed the 61 belts all hanging in Sir's storeroom, he felt pleased and proud. Not only was he the first elephant in the forest with a manager, but he was undoubtedly the first elephant who had ever made 61 belts. Of course, he had had some help from Sir Augustus, but he had done most of the work himself. Now if he could only build the trampoline and master his flip, he'd be the proudest elephant of all.

After a delicious dinner of fricasseed bamboo shoots and grass cakes which Sir Augustus cooked, Elliott went home to his little house and went straight to bed. He slept very soundly and dreamt of magnificent feats on the trampoline. The next morning he woke

up early, got dressed, had breakfast and rushed over to Sir Augustus's house. He knocked cheerfully on the door. But there was no answer. He should have known! It was much too early for Sir to be up and about.

So Elliott sat in the sun and spun dreams of glory in which he became the richest and most famous elephant of all. He didn't really care much about money, but if he had a lot of money, then he could help poor elephants and travel and do ever so many things. He was quite absorbed in these pleasant thoughts and so he didn't even notice Sir Augustus until he bellowed at him.

"Hey, boy! What are you doing? Indeed what ARE you doing . . . lounging around when we have so much to do? Get up boy, Let's be at it." Elliott started to explain that he'd been waiting over two hours for Sir to get up, but he realized it would be useless. Arguing with someone older is usually a big waste of time. They know more words and can talk louder and think up arguments faster than you can.

"Okay, Sir. Let's go. Can we start trading the belts for suspenders now? Shall we each take a different section of the forest, or shall we go together? Shall we . . ."

Sir interrupted. "Hold on, boy. Hold on! Come inside. We have to discuss our plans calmly and carefully like adults. Come in. We'll have a cup of tea and talk it over."

Sir Augustus brought the tea to the table and sat down heavily as if he planned to be there for a long, long time. All day long, Elliott thought.

Sir took a very large swallow of tea and drew himself up and said sternly: "We need a plan, boy, a plan. After all, we want to trade 61 vine belts for 61 pairs of suspenders. That's an audacious scheme, my boy, a very audacious scheme."

Elliott didn't know what "audacious" meant but it sounded awful! "Yes, Sir."

"To accomplish this, we have to persuade our friends that belts are BETTER than suspenders. We'll have to explain that they are more modern, as you suggested, and more dashing, too. Now, you know as well as I do, that if there's ANYTHING a self-respecting elephant wants to be it's DASHING! DASHING, my boy, dashing."

Elliott began to get excited by Sir's talk. "Yes, Sir Augustus. Yes!" He began to picture himself as the elephant who made all the other elephants in the forest more dashing. He liked the role immediately.

"My boy, I'll tell you a secret. I'd hate for this to get out to my British friends, but belts are infinitely more comfortable than braces. There's not all that pulling at the shoulder blades, not all that tugging and pinching. And, my boy, elephants love to be comfortable almost as much as they love to be dashing. So, my boy, those are the points we'll stress — our belts are dashing, comfortable and

41

modern." With that, Sir Augustus stood up, waved his arm and shouted: "Onward!"

"Sir, would you mind if we started out together, so I can sort of see how you persuade them to trade? I'm not sure I can keep all that straight about dashing and modern and comfortable."

Sir Augustus was very pleased, so pleased that he almost smiled. Instead he said gruffly: "Not at all, my boy. Not at all. It's a sound idea . . . a VERY sound idea. Come along with me, you'll get the hang of it soon enough. And remember, my boy, remember THINK POSITIVE."

And so Elliott and Sir Augustus gathered up as many belts as they could carry and set out.

It was a lovely day. The sky was very, very blue and the air was cool and clear and the sun was bright. Elliott thought that it was definitely a high-hopeful day . . . a fine day for belt-peddling.

The first elephants they met were Alphie, Otto and Skeets, three tough young elephants. Elliott had always avoided them, because they made fun of his size, laughed at him and called him "Peewee." He would have preferred to avoid them this time. He didn't think meeting them was a good omen for belt-peddling. But Sir called to them.

Alphie, Otto and Skeets were obviously quite in awe of Sir and came right over. "Hello, Sir, did you call us?" Alphie said, ignoring Elliott.

"Indeed, I did. Nice day, isn't it, boys? Beautiful day, in fact. I have something here I thought you might be interested in. You seem to be bright, forward-thinking boys. Just thought you might be interested."

Elliott watched Sir. He was really very smart. He had already made it clear that if the boys weren't interested in the belts, they would appear stupid and backward. Elliott knew that no elephant, especially a tough

43

young elephant, wants to appear stupid and backward.

"What's that, Sir?" Otto asked eagerly.

"Belts, my boys. Belts."

"Belts?" they said in a chorus.

"Belts! Take a look at these fine belts we have here. Suspenders are old-fashioned, uncomfortable, definitely undashing. But belts . . . BELTS, my boys, are modern, comfortable and dashing."

Alphie, Skeets and Otto looked VERY interested. Otto was self-consciously plucking at his suspenders.

Sir Augustus went on. "And these belts, these snappy, modern, comfortable, dashing belts . . . these brand-new belts won't cost you a thing. Not a thing. We'll do you a favor, in fact. A big favor. We'll give you each a terrific belt and we'll dispose of your suspenders for you."

Otto already had his suspenders off. He handed them to Sir Augustus.

But Alphie was frowning. He said: "Wait. Wait a minute, Otto." He turned to Sir Augustus. "Why are you being so nice? Why do you care whether we look dashing and modern? Why have you and the runt gone to all this trouble for us? What's in it for you?"

Elliott flinched at the word "runt" and his heart began to thud in his chest. What would Sir say, he wondered? He knew it was a bad omen when they met the three young toughs.

Sir Augustus drew himself up to his full height and glowered at Alphie. "No need to be rude, my boy. No need at all. Good manners suffice in any situation. What's in it for us, you ask? Dreadful expression! Dreadful! You're suspicious. You're afraid we're putting something over on you . . ." He rolled his eyes dramatically.

"Well, boys . . . in a way, you're right. I do need your suspenders and that's why I wanted to trade you the belts. But . . . " he paused and sighed.

46

Oh-oh, Elliott thought. Here it comes. Now he's going to tell them about the trampoline and Alphie and Otto and Skeets will tell all the other elephants and it'll be the joke of the forest. And that'll be that.

Sir went on, "The one thing in this world that I want is a hammock. Yes. I'm getting old and I want a hammock to rest in." Elliott was astonished and very impressed. Sir had made a great sacrifice. He had admitted that he was getting old, rather than give away Elliott's secret. Elliott was very grateful and very proud of Sir.

Otto and Alphie and Skeets were plainly very impressed by Sir's story. They shuffled about and looked embarrassed and mumbled that they'd be happy to trade their darn old suspenders for modern belts.

Sir Augustus spoke very slowly. "Here are your belts, boys." He was very proud and serious.

Alphie and Skeets took off their suspenders

and took the belts. They thanked Sir and nodded at Elliott and put on the belts. Skeets said: "Gee, Sir Augustus, these belts are . . . well . . . modern and they certainly are comfortable. Thanks again, Sir. Gee, thanks." They went off down the trail quietly.

Sir Augustus sighed an immense sigh. "Whew! Well, my boy, that was a close one. I'd hate to go through that again. And I want to point out that I didn't tell a lie. I didn't actually say that we were going to MAKE a hammock of the suspenders. I said I *wanted* a hammock. They concluded we were going to make the hammock out of the suspenders. Fancy bit of thinking there, my boy. A regular ballet of the brain. Lying is bad, boy. Very bad. Leading elephants to conclusions . . . that's art, boy."

Elliott couldn't see the difference, but he supposed that he would understand it when he was older. Anyway, he was happy that

Sir Augustus hadn't had to give away their secret. Besides, whatever Sir had done, and Elliott wasn't quite sure what he had done, he'd done for Elliott.

After the terrible time with Otto, Skeets and Alphie, the rest of the day went smoothly. Sir Augustus did most of the talking . . . well, in fact, all of the talking . . . and Elliott passed out the belts and carried the suspenders. Nearly all the elephants they met were happy to trade their suspenders for modern, comfortable, dashing belts. Only a few stuffy, old elephants grumped and said suspenders were good enough for them. At 5 P.M., Sir said that they'd done quite enough for one day and suggested that they go back for some tea.

As they walked back to Sir's house, he talked elatedly: "Well, my boy, after that bad beginning with those young toughs, it's been a good day, a very good day. Very soon we'll have enough suspenders to make your trampoline.

I'm looking forward to that. Then we can relax."

Elliott realized that Sir could relax, but his work would just be beginning. When the trampoline was built, he'd have to learn to do a flip. Suddenly he wasn't sure that he'd be able to master it. He was plunged into gloom. Wouldn't that be awful? Sir would be FURIOUS! Well, it didn't bear thinking about. He'd simply have to do it!

Back at Sir's house, the old elephant put a kettle of water on the fire and they sorted out the belts and suspenders.

They had collected half of the suspenders they needed for the trampoline in one day. That was a good omen. Elliott believed in omens, though he wasn't quite sure what they were. Sort of like lucky stones, he thought.

Sir poured the tea and settled heavily down at the table. "I want to make a toast, my boy. To you and your trampoline." He raised his cup and drank noisily. "If we work hard tomorrow, we should be able to gather up the rest of the suspenders. Then . . . THEN . . . we can start work on the trampoline. That'll be terribly exciting. I think I'll make a banner, too. It'll say 'Sir Augustus presents Elliott the Elephant doing various astonishing feats on the trampoline.' How does that sound?"

"Well, I think it's a little too long. And it sounds a little too grand, too. After all, I'm just going to do a flip . . . ," he paused, "maybe . . ."

"No 'maybes' about it, my boy! You HAVE to do a flip. Otherwise all our work will have been for nothing."

Somehow, Sir's reasoning seemed backwards to Elliott, but he didn't say anything. He just stared into his tea and thought about taking the tea leaves to Mama Monkey so she could read his fortune. On the other hand, he'd rather not know. No sense in facing bad news before you had to.

"Well, son, let's not talk about it. Let's do it. You hurry home now and get a good night's sleep, so we can start out bright and early in the morning."

So Elliott, who suddenly felt very sleepy, ran home through the forest and went straight to bed and dreamed about doing double flips and triple flips and QUADRUPLE flips on his trampoline. It was such a nice dream . . . his high, looping flips were so beautiful, so graceful and all the elephants — even Alphie, Otto and Skeets — were cheering so heartily . . . that he overslept! When he woke it was nearly ten o'clock. Heavens! He pulled his clothes on, splashed some water in his face and ran as fast as he could to Sir Augustus's house.

Sir Augustus was standing in the doorway shouting at about 30 elephants. Elliott pushed through them and went up to Sir Augustus. "What's going on?" he said. "What's happening here?"

Sir looked down: "Oh, my boy, glad to see

you. Where've you been? I've been up for hours . . . since dawn. These elephants all want to trade their suspenders for belts. That's what's going on. They saw the ones we traded yesterday and rushed right over here. We've started a trend, my boy, a trend. Give me a hand, boy, help me hand out these belts."

Elliott wasn't sure what a trend was, but it didn't sound like a bad thing to start. So he took a handful of belts and began passing them out to the elephants. More and more elephants appeared. By noon they had traded all the belts for suspenders, and the elephants went off through the forest, looking very pleased with themselves and their belts.

Elliott and Sir Augustus began sorting through the tangle of suspenders. Sir said triumphantly: "My boy, there's nothing so powerful as an idea whose time has come." Elliott looked confused. Sir said, "I didn't make that up, boy. Someone else did. Can't remember who right now. Anyway, the point

is that the elephants in the forest were READY for belts. We just got here at the right time. Pity we didn't sell them. Why, we would have made a fortune. We could have taken a holiday at the seashore. Pity."

Elliott said: "But, Sir, if we'd sold them, then we wouldn't have gotten the suspenders. And if we didn't have the suspenders, we couldn't make a trampoline. And without a trampoline, I can't do my flip. And . . ."

"Yes. Yes. You're right, my boy. I got carried away with our success. Mustn't ever get carried away. Moderation in all things, my boy. Even enthusiasm."

"What shall we do now, Sir?" Elliott didn't want to appear too enthusiastic, but he was very anxious to begin work on the trampoline.

But Sir Augustus said: "Let's have lunch, boy. Can't think on an empty stomach and it's been an exhausting morning. I'll go make some tea, you pick some grapes and ivy leaves.

Then we can make our plans. Hurry, boy, we haven't a minute to waste."

Elliott suddenly felt very cheerful and quickly gathered up some grapes and ivy leaves. He hoped that Sir wouldn't want to take a nap after lunch.

After a very satisfying lunch, Elliott washed the dishes and then sat down at the table with Sir Augustus. "Now what, Sir? What shall we do now?"

Sir snorted: "Now, my boy, NOW we build the trampoline so that you can start practicing your flips . . . My boy, we have to get cracking. After all, I can't spend the rest of my life helping you. I have lots of very important projects of my own. So let's get busy. We'll take the suspenders up to the clearing on the cliff. There's a hammer and some nails in the closet over there. Oh, and we'll need a saw. Do you have a saw, boy?"

Elliott sighed: "No, Sir, but I have two dollars and fifty-nine cents saved up in my little silver bank. We could use that to buy one."

"Boy, if your money's in the bank, how do you know how much money you have? I mean, if the bank is silver, you can't see through it. And if you can't see through it, how in the world do you know how much money you have in it? Come now, boy!"

Elliott looked surprised. "Well, Sir, I've kept track of every penny I've put in on this little piece of paper. And it says $2.59."

Sir said dubiously, "Well, we'll see, boy. We'll see how accurate that piece of paper is. Go get your little silver bank, boy. And we'll

see. Pop to. Hurry, boy, we've got a lot to do."

So Elliott ran through the forest as fast as he could to his house and got the bank. He shook it. It certainly SOUNDED like $2.59. Then he got the tiny key out from under his teapot. Since he used the teapot a lot, it wasn't a very good place to hide the key, but it had been the best place he could think of. Then he ran back through the forest, the bank jingling merrily. He was quite out of breath when he got to Sir's house.

Sir looked at the bank curiously. "My, that's a handsome little bank. Now let's open it quickly."

Elliott put the key in the lock and turned it. The bank popped open and Elliott poured the money out on the table.

Sir moved forward and said: "I'll count, my boy. I'm a very good counter. I'm a wizard at higher mathematics. $X + Y = XY$. How's that, boy?"

Elliott had no idea what Sir was talking

about, but he smiled and said: "That's terrific, Sir, really terrific. Shall we count the money?"

"Yes, my boy. Yes indeed. Now let's see. You have 15 dimes. One dime is worth 10 cents. So that's one dollar and fifty cents. Good start, my boy. Now, let's see, eleven nickels, that's fifty-five cents. That's a total of $2.05. And fifty-four pennies, that's 54 cents. And $2.05 and 54 is . . . my heavens . . . $2.59. You're right, my boy, you're right. $2.59. Now the only problem is whether we can buy a saw for $2.59. Let's go down to the saw shop and see."

They gathered up the suspenders and the hammer and nails and set off to the saw shop which was down the road and over the hill from Sir Augustus's house. Mr. Mangrove, who ran the saw shop, was a very large elephant. He was known in the forest for his strength and his bad temper. If he chose to, he could probably throw Elliott halfway across the forest. So Elliott was very glad that

Sir was going with him to see Mr. Mangrove. They arrived at the shop and it was filled with beautiful shiny saws of all sizes. Surely there was one which was only $2.59. They went in.

Mr. Mangrove was sitting in front of a huge book with a lot of numbers in it. He looked in a bad mood. Sir went right up to him: "Mr. Mangrove, my dear sir, it's nice to see you. How have you been?"

"Terrible. Terrible. I have had a head cold for three weeks. And it's not getting any better." He frowned and looked very fierce. Elliott stood close behind Sir Augustus. "Well, what do you want? I don't suppose you stopped by just to inquire about my health. Out with it. What do you want?" He grunted and sniffed.

Sir drew himself grandly up to his full height. "As a matter of fact, we want to buy a saw. Not just any saw. A special saw. And of course, when anyone in the forest thinks of saws, they naturally think of you. As . . ."

Mr. Mangrove interrupted rudely: "Of course, you thought of me. Who else sells saws in the forest? Come now, let's not waste time. Out with it! What sort of saw do you want?"

"Well, we want a fine saw . . . a very special saw. A saw that's shiny and sharp . . . a saw that will cut through the hardest wood. A saw that is nice to hold. A saw that sparkles and . . ."

Mr. Mangrove broke in again: "How much do you have to spend? That's the important thing . . . that'll decide what kind of saw you get. How much actual cash do you have?" Elliott thought he was quite the rudest man he'd ever met and stood closer to Sir Augustus.

Sir was magnificent. He looked Mr. Mangrove right in the eye and said: "We have $2.59 which should be enough to buy an entirely adequate saw. After all, we're not going into the business of sawing; we simply

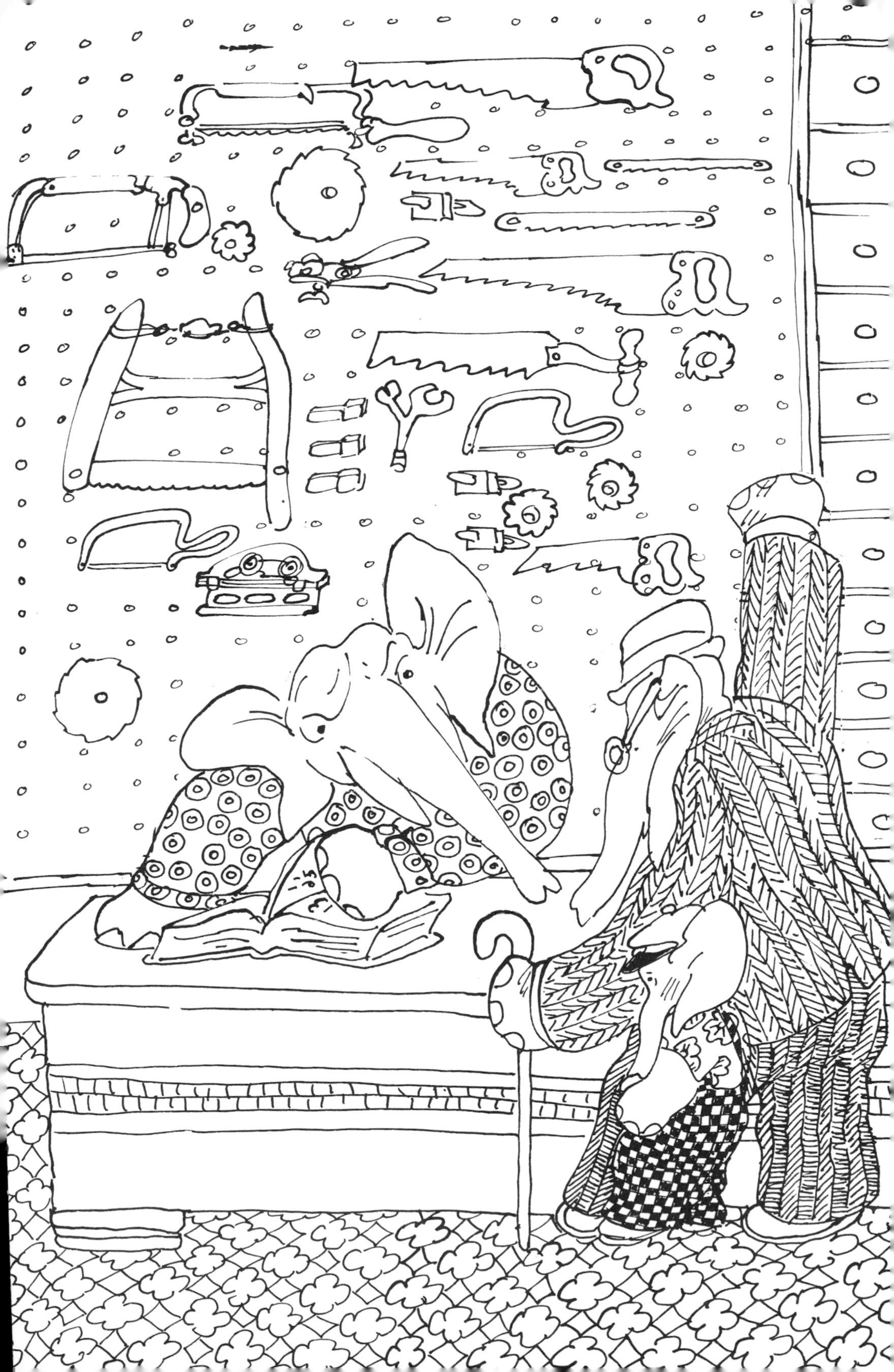

have a few things which we want to saw today."

Mr. Mangrove was a little nicer all of a sudden. He said: "Oh, $2.59. Well, for $2.59 I could sell you that smallish saw over there." He pointed at a small and pitiful saw which didn't look as if it would cut cardboard. And it certainly wouldn't cut mahogany. But Mr. Mangrove added: "For $2.59, I could rent you that splendid shiny saw over there for 24 hours. Would that give you enough time to finish all of your sawing?" It was a fine, big saw.

Sir was still looking rather grand, but he winked at Elliott. "Indeed, Mr. Mangrove, that would be adequate for our needs." His voice was very cold and his manner very royal. "But $2.59 seems a lot of money for one day's use."

Sir waved his trunk haughtily. "Why, that's more than 10 cents an hour. And, of course, we have to sleep. And, of course, we can't saw in the dark. So that leaves us about eight hours of sawing time. And that's more than 30 cents an hour. That's OUTRAGEOUS!!" Sir was practically shouting. Elliott thought that he had never known anyone quite so grand and brave in his whole life.

Sir went on: "My dear sir, I should think that your own conscience would pain you exquisitely. If you would extract $2.59 from us for the mere rental of a saw for eight hours of sawing, you deserve your head cold! I never heard of anything so outrageous in my life! Elliott, let's leave immediately."

They turned and started out of the saw shop, but Mr. Mangrove was on their heels, practically begging them to reconsider. "Please, Sir, I didn't mean the WHOLE $2.59 for the renting. I meant only . . . well, maybe . . . 80 cents." Elliott was very glad that he was reconsidering, as he really couldn't imagine how he and Sir could build a proper trampoline without a saw.

Sir thought for a minute. "Hmmm. Well, I suppose 80 cents is reasonable enough. We'll take it. Give him eighty cents, my boy." Mr. Mangrove looked very tired and unhappy. Elliott counted out eight dimes and gave them to Mr. Mangrove. He got the beautiful saw and gave it to Elliott and said: "Thank you very much. I'm sorry about that little misunderstanding. I think I'll take a nap now. I'm a little tired. Good luck on your project . . . whatever your project is." He went through a door at the back of his shop and closed it.

"Haha, my boy! Outsmarted him, didn't we? Can you imagine? $2.59 to rent a saw! Outrageous! Mangrove has a very mean nature."

Elliott smiled at Sir and thought he was simply fine. "Well, Sir, you certainly didn't let him get away with anything."

Sir puffed up a little and looked very proud. "Well, boy, I've been around. I've traveled a lot. I've met a lot of elephants like that. Always trying to get away with something. They look down on other elephants. Have no respect for them. Very bad way to be. Always try to be nice. Always try to be fair. Always try to be helpful. Those are good rules, boy."

Elliott nodded: "Yes, Sir. Those are certainly good rules to follow."

Sir grunted: "Of course, they are, boy. Of course, they are. There's a lifetime of thinking in those rules. A lifetime . . ."

Elliott suspected that Sir had just thought them up, but he just nodded.

Sir waved grandly and said: "Let's be off. Let's hurry up to the clearing on the cliff and start work. After all, we can't keep the saw forever. We agreed to return it tomorrow."

Elliott was very excited. They were actually going to build the trampoline! He felt as if he'd been waiting all his life for this moment. So they hurried through the forest and up the path to the clearing on the cliff. It was a steep, winding path and since it was very seldom used, it was overgrown with plants and bushes. About halfway up, Sir stopped so suddenly that Elliott crashed right into him.

Sir turned angrily. "Watch it, boy! What do you think you're doing? Just crashed right into me." He was breathing very hard.

"I'm sorry, Sir. I really am sorry. I guess I was too busy thinking about the trampoline to watch where I was going. I hope I didn't hurt you." Elliott felt very stupid.

"NO, of course you didn't hurt me! After all, I'm quite a bit bigger than you are. It's the principle of the thing. You just shouldn't go around running into people. It's not good manners."

Elliott said, "I'm sorry, Sir. I'm very sorry. I really am."

Sir nodded, "Well, don't do it again," and marched briskly up the path. Keeping a careful eye on him, in case he stopped, Elliott walked behind Sir. In a few minutes' time, they got to the clearing on the cliff. Sir sat down on a log and breathed deeply. "Well, my boy, this is it. Here we are. My, my, it's quite beautiful up here." Elliott looked around. It was beautiful. It was rather as if they were on a raft, sailing over a sea of treetops. A cool breeze was playing in the tall grass.

Sir gazed about. He said: "We elephants are very silly. We live in the forest because elephants always live in the forest. It's a tradition. Elephants live in the forest. We should live up here, my boy. Cool breeze and lovely view. Elephants stick too much to tradition. They should break away, do new things, explore, look around.

"But if elephants want to be dull, they'll be dull, that's their nature. Very stubborn creatures. Let's pick the location for the trampoline. How about over there?" He walked about ten feet away and gestured. "This is a beautiful spot. If you're not inspired

to do a flip here, you'll NEVER do one."
Elliott walked over to Sir. It was a fine spot.
One could see for miles over the top of the
forest and, far, far away, some mountains rose
up like the edge of a huge saw. "Sir. This is
a wonderful spot. A beautiful view and cool
breezes. Oh, it's a grand spot for a trampoline."

Sir beamed. "Glad you like it, boy. Yes, it's
perfect." He began pacing around. "Let's
pace out the trampoline. Now, we want it
to be nine feet long. That's three yards. Each
pace is a yard, so we want it to be three paces
long. You get some twigs to pound in at the
corners."

Elliott was very excited and ran over to
a tree and broke off four twigs. When he got
back, Sir was standing like a statue. "Now
stick one here. Right between my feet."

Elliott stuck the twig into the ground between Sir's feet and Sir paced out three yards.
"Now here, boy. Another twig here." Elliott

ran over and stuck another twig in the ground.
"Now, boy. We want it five feet wide. A foot
is a foot. So we'll use my foot. Your foot is
probably not quite a foot." Sir was very
amused by himself.

Starting at the twig, Sir carefully — and
Elliott had to admit — quite gracefully measured out five feet. "Another twig, my boy,
another twig." Elliott stuck another twig
in the ground. Then Sir paced off three yards
and Elliott stuck another twig in the ground.
Sir stepped back and said: "There, my boy,
there's your trampoline. Magnificent, isn't it?"
All Elliott could see was four twigs stuck in
the ground, but it was a start. "What now,
Sir?"

"Now we build the frame out of the sturdiest
mahogany logs we can find. We need one tree
28 feet tall and about a foot through. Or two
smaller trees. Let's start looking, boy. You
go that way, I'll go this way."

Elliott went to the edge of the clearing and

into the trees. Most of the trees were either entirely too big or much too small. Some were old and cracking with age. Others were slender and green. After tramping around for a while, he got very discouraged. There was no such thing as a perfect trampoline tree, he thought. Sir was just being unusually optimistic, expecting to find one tree that they could make an entire trampoline out of.

Elliott wandered through the trees aimlessly, not really paying much attention and suddenly he saw a perfect tree. It was very tall and bigger around than Sir's leg. He called out: "Sir, Sir. I found it. I found the perfect trampoline tree. Over here, Sir. Look at this."

It was really a beautiful tree and Elliott was suddenly quite sad. It would be terrible to cut down such a fine tree. But he heard a great crashing off to his left and then a call. "I'm coming, boy. I'm coming."

Suddenly he saw Sir rushing through the trees, knocking small bushes aside as he walked. Elliott thought it was lucky that they were tree-hunting, because trees don't have ears. If they had been hunting for lions — which was exceedingly unlikely, because as a rule elephants do not go looking for lions — every lion in the forest would have heard them.

Sir skidded to a stop by Elliott and said, breathlessly: "Where is it, boy? Where's the perfect tree. I had begun to think there was no such thing. In fact, I was getting very discouraged. I had thought that lots of trees would probably do for us. But the ones I saw were too tall, too short, too old, too young, too green, too brittle, something wrong with all of them. Where is it, boy?"

Elliott proudly pointed at the tree. Sir had been discouraged, too. Somehow, when you feel discouraged, you think that you're the only one who's discouraged. He would try to remember that the next time he was discouraged.

Sir looked at the tree very thoroughly. He

seemed to be measuring it with his eye, squinting and tilting his head.

He didn't say anything for a long time and Elliott began to get discouraged again. He thought that Sir didn't like it, after all. He thought that it wasn't a perfect tree. He had just begun to think that it was a terrible tree, when Sir spoke: "My boy, you are right. This is a fine tree. Tall and straight and at least a foot through the middle." Elliott felt happy again. "But how on earth are we going to move it?" He shrugged helplessly. Elliott's heart sank. He actually felt it sink inside him, like a stone sinks in water. Plomp!

Sir waved wildly at the tree. "Look at it! Just what we need. Perfect, as you said. An altogether ideal tree! But here it is in the midst of the forest. We need it out there in the clearing where our twigs are. Doesn't do us a bit of good here. Can't do a thing with it."

"But, Sir," Elliott was not sure what he was going to say, but he didn't want Sir to lose heart in the whole project now. "But, Sir, why don't we . . ."

"What, boy? What? If you have an idea, share it with me. What we need just now is a good idea. What?"

Suddenly, Elliott knew. "Sir, if we cut it down here, it'll *fall* over there! And then we can cut it up and put each piece in place and nail it together and I'll have a trampoline and . . ."

Sir interrupted. "Slow down, boy. Slow down. Good thinking. If we saw it here at the right angle, it will fall over there. Capital thinking! But let's do that before we make any more plans. Get the saw quickly, we haven't a moment to waste. It must be tea-time."

Elliott ran and got the saw and brought it back. Sir Augustus, by that time, had figured out that if they sawed the tree trunk on the side away from the clearing, it would fall towards the clearing. "We'll saw on this side, boy. And we'll take turns. Sawing is very tiring work, I think. I'm older and larger, so I'll start."

Sir grasped the saw with great determination and stood firmly, feet apart. He laid the cutting side against the tree and Elliott said in a quiet voice: "Good-bye, old tree. You will be proud of me one day."

Sir paused. "What did you say, boy?"

"Nothing, I was just sort of mumbling out loud."

Sir turned back to the tree and started to saw. He began very fast, sawing, going to and fro against the tree and, it seemed to Elliott, making hardly a mark. In a minute, Sir was breathing very hard. He stopped suddenly and said: "Your turn, boy."

Elliott stepped up to the tree and took the saw. He could barely see where Sir had sawed. Slow but sure, he thought, was the way to saw down a tree. And so he pushed the saw into the bark of the tree and pulled it toward him . . . slowly and surely. He had made a small cut in the tree. Balancing the saw in the cut, he pushed it, he pulled it. Push . . . pull . . . push . . . pull. Sawdust was piling up in a little mound on the ground. It was hard work, but Elliott rather enjoyed it. He felt that he was really doing something. Push . . . pull . . . push . . . pull. More sawdust. He had cut in about three inches. It was a fine saw, he thought. He had forgotten about Sir.

But suddenly Sir shouted: "Enough, boy. Enough. My turn. My turn. You're a fine sawer. Slow, but sure. I'll take over now." Sir took the saw and Elliott sat down.

This time, Sir was much slower and more patient. It made Elliott quite sleepy to watch the saw going slowly, slowly back and forth. It seemed that Sir simply wasn't a very good sawer. After very little progress, he summoned Elliott back to the saw. "It's your turn, boy.

Now really go at it this time. Let's see some real progress."

Elliott went eagerly back to the saw. They were about four inches in by now. Eight inches to go. Now sawdust was piling up all around the base of the tree. And he sawed and sawed and sawed. Push . . . pull . . . push . . . pull. Push . . . pull. Push . . . pull. Push-pull. Pushpull. Pushpull. His muscles began to sing out. And twinge. Pushpull. Pushpull. Pushpull. And suddenly the whole forest shook and Elliott fell down. He had sawed right through without knowing it and the tree had crashed to the ground.

Sir had been dozing, probably put to sleep by the bzzzzzz of the saw, but he leapt to his feet. "What's happening, boy? What's going on? What was that terrible crash?"

Elliott pointed at the tree and got up. "The tree. We cut it down. I didn't even know it." He felt tired, but excited.

"Stupendous, my boy. Simply stupendous."
Sir seemed quite refreshed from his little nap.
"Now we'll build your trampoline."

Elliott agreed. He was very excited.

Sir walked the length of the fallen tree and
back. It had lots of branches. "First, we'll
have to saw all the branches off. It should be
as smooth as possible." Elliott said eagerly:
"I'll saw them off, Sir. I really enjoy sawing.
It's so sort of peaceful. Bzzzzzzing away."

Sir could barely hide his delight. "All right,
boy, if you want to. While you're sawing, I'll
measure out the sections we'll need to make
the trampoline. On second thought, I think
we'll have *six* legs and four side pieces and
two end pieces. That way it'll be sturdier.
You can flip higher than ever. Besides, I think
it'll be easier to build."

Elliott began sawing the branches off. He
had the hang of sawing now and the branches
weren't nearly so thick as the tree itself. He

sawed . . . and sawed and tried to keep his trunk out of the little piles of sawdust, because it made him feel like sneezing. Sneezing wouldn't do. Sir would get very angry if Elliott started sneezing.

Meanwhile, Sir was making mysterious marks on the tree with a nail. Elliott couldn't understand how he was measuring at first and then he noticed that he was measuring the tree in hammer-lengths.

When Elliott had sawed all the branches off the tree, he suddenly noticed that the sun was very low in the West. In an hour it would be dark and they'd have to stop. He called out: "Sir, do you think we can build the trampoline before the sun sets? It's almost into the mountains."

Sir looked up from his marking. He glanced at the sun and then at Elliott: "Of course, boy, of course. We have to. Now you start sawing where I've made the nail-marks. You'll be surprised. Why, we'll have it built long before the sun goes down. We've already done all of the hard part. Start sawing, boy, and be quick."

Elliott felt full of twinges, little pullings inside. But the more he sawed, the easier it was. So he sawed and sawed and sawed. Twelve times he sawed through the tree and each time the piece he had just sawed went CHONK on the ground.

Finally, he finished. He felt very proud of himself. Elliott the smallest elephant of all had cut down a huge tree and then cut it up into short pieces. He hoped that Sir Augustus had measured correctly. For Elliott had really sawed enough for one day. He called to Sir, who was still muttering and pacing around the twigs they'd put in the ground. "Sir, Sir, I'm finished. It's all cut up. Just where you marked it. I sawed at all the places you marked and I'm finished now."

Sir looked annoyed and shouted back: "All right. All right. Patience, my boy.

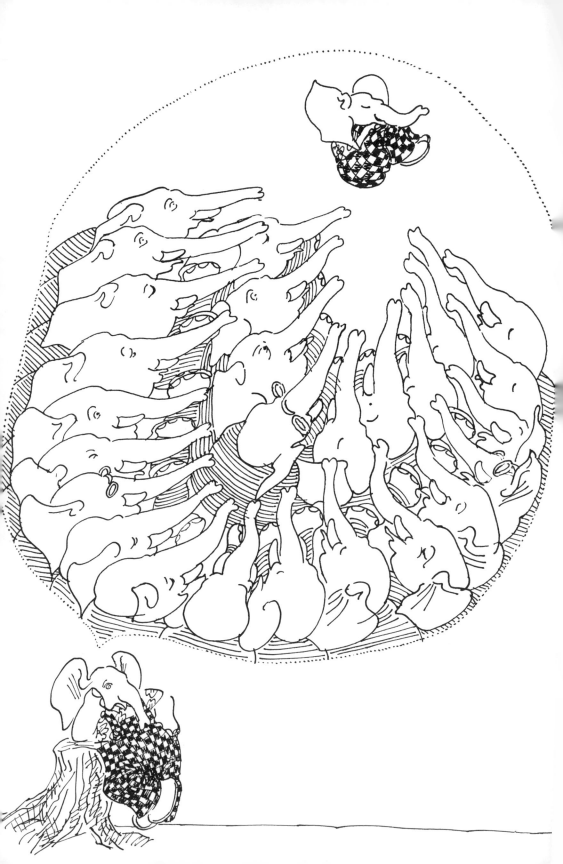

There's more to building a trampoline than sawing, my boy. Lots more. I'll be there in a minute."

Elliott leaned on the tree stump and closed his eyes. The light was already full of shadows and the air felt pleasant and cool on his face. He thought about the day when he would do his flip on the trampoline in front of all the other elephants. He thought how wonderful it would be to be flying through the air ever so gracefully and look down at all the upturned faces of the other elephants. The hurrays and clapping had just begun when Sir nudged him with the hammer. "Come, boy, no time for dreaming now. Let's roll the pieces out to the clearing."

Luckily the floor of the forest was surprisingly smooth, so they were able to roll the sawed up pieces of the tree out without much trouble. Of course, Elliott had sawed off the branches so neatly that the stumps didn't snag in the bushes. Elliott thought that if, for some

reason, he couldn't master the flip, he could always take up sawing as a career.

Soon all the funny-looking logs were in the clearing next to the twigs they'd stuck in the ground. Sir said: "All right. I'll put the legs of the trampoline in place. Don't wilt now, boy, we're nearly finished." Very carefully, Sir rolled each log into place and put it on its end. Elephants — even small ones — were really terribly good at rolling things.

Sir sat down on each log after it was in place to sort of secure it to the ground. Then he announced. "Now we'll put the end-pieces on. Get the hammer and nails. Be quick, boy. I'd hate to build anything as tricky as a trampoline in the dark."

Elliott got the nails and hammer and by the time he turned around, Sir had one end-piece in place on the legs. "Quick, boy. Quick. Hammer it on."

Elliott was so used to sawing that hammering was hard at first, but he finally had nailed

85

both ends in place. Then they did the other
end. Sir put the first side-piece in place and
Elliott nailed it on. Then the second. And
the third. And the fourth. Then, for good
measure, he nailed the end-pieces to the side-
pieces. It certainly *looked* very sturdy . . .
and reliable.

At that moment, the sun vanished behind the mountains and it was suddenly dark. Sir whispered noisily, "Let's hide the suspenders and the hammer and nails here and hurry home before it gets any darker." Elliott couldn't imagine that it could be any darker than it was, but he hid everything in an old rabbit hole under a bush on the edge of the clearing and they started home. Elliott had the impression that Sir Augustus didn't like the dark any better than he did. He clutched onto the saw and pretended it was a giant sword and followed Sir down the path.

Sir was moving along quite smartly and Elliott stayed as close to him as possible. He didn't want to bump into him again. Suddenly, Sir Augustus lurched forward and nearly lost his balance. Elliott called out: "Sir, Sir, what's happening? Are you all right, Sir? What's happening?"

"Hush, boy. Hush! Let me catch my breath." They had stopped on the path and

it was very quiet. There wasn't a sound any-
where. Elliott shivered, even though it wasn't
cold. He wished that Sir would say something.

"Nothing happened. I simply tripped on
a rock. Lost my balance. Almost fell down.
It's just lucky that I have natural grace. Otherwise, I might have rolled all the way down
the path, gotten all battered and bruised.
Now WATCH YOUR STEP, BOY. Watch
where you're going." And he turned and
started down the path again.

Elliott found that as his eyes adjusted to
the dark, he wasn't so scared. Actually, it was
very pleasant walking along in the quiet.
It was peaceful. Elliott and Sir had had a
long and exciting day and Elliott was ex-
hausted. He was quite ready for bed, but he
knew that he wouldn't sleep much. He was
too excited about actually finishing the trampoline tomorrow and starting to learn his flip.

Finally, they were off the path and back in

their own forest. It was as familiar as their own backyards, and they walked quickly through the trees. "Elliott, run home now and get a good night's sleep. In the morning, when you wake up, take the saw back to Mr. Mangrove and thank him for his generosity. Then come by my house and we'll go back up the cliff. Good night, boy. Sweet dreams."

Elliott hurried home, had some supper and went to bed. He felt very tired, but he couldn't go to sleep. He kept thinking about the trampoline and about his flip. What would happen if he couldn't do the flip? Well, Sir would be awfully mad, for one thing. Elliott himself would be heartbroken. It would be awful . . . after all this planning and work . . . if he COULDN'T do the flip. Well, he WOULD do it . . . that was that. And then Elliott fell asleep and dreamed all night of doing his flip, flying above the elephants, looking down at their surprised faces.

In fact, his dreams were so pleasant that Elliott overslept. It was mid-morning when he woke up and he dressed quickly and had some tea and grapes and ran over to Mr. Mangrove's to return the saw. Mr. Mangrove was sitting in front of his shop, sharpening saws and Elliott went up to him and said: "Here's your saw. Thank you very much."

Mr. Mangrove looked up and grunted. He looked mean and seemed to be in a bad mood, so Elliott said, "Thank you again" and ran off toward Sir's house.

When Elliott got to Sir's house, he was out of breath and his muscles were twinging again. That was from the sawing, he thought. He knocked on Sir's door. From inside, he heard "Who's that? Just a minute. Stop that pounding! I'm coming, I'm coming." Elliott hadn't pounded, he had just knocked a perfectly normal knock. He HOPED Sir wasn't in one of his bad moods.

Suddenly, the door flew open and there stood Sir, holding a cup of tea. He had a very fierce expression on his face. But on seeing Elliott, he didn't look quite so fierce. "Oh, it's you, boy. Come in, come in. Elephants have been knocking on the door all morning . . . prying into our affairs . . . asking silly questions . . . trying to sell me things. There was even a group of elephants from another part of the forest who wanted to sell me their suspenders. Elephants are the nosiest animals in the world." He laughed and looked at Elliott. "That's a joke, my boy. A rather good one, too. You see, our trunks are noses and they are certainly the biggest noses in the world. That makes us the nosiest animals . . . well, not us in particular . . . all elephants."

Elliott laughed quietly. He'd never seen Sir in such a good mood. "What kind of questions were they asking, Sir?"

"Well, they wanted to know what we were

doing. They all know that we're doing SOME-THING, but they're not sure what. Now then, shall we be off to the trampoline?"

"Oh, yes, Sir. I can't wait to start practicing my flip."

"Practicing? PRACTICING? You have to learn how to do it first, boy. First things first. Well, I'll just put my teacup in the sink and we'll go. Did you take the saw back to Mr. Mangrove?"

"Yes, Sir. I wonder if we shouldn't take some lunch up to the cliff. That way, we can stay up there longer."

"Capital idea, boy. Capital. We'll take a bottle of tea. There's some on the stove. It's all made. Just pour it into that bottle. Then we'll take some grapes and ivy leaves. That is a good idea." Sir put the food in a paper bag and Elliott put the bottle of tea under his arm and they set out for the trampoline.

It was a beautiful day. The sun was shining, slanting down through the trees in delicate columns of light. The birds were singing and a cool breeze played through the trees. Elliott had high hopes for this day. This MIGHT be the day that he did his first flip. On the other hand, it might not. Elliott felt superstitious about hoping too much or predicting things. It was better, he thought, simply to do your best.

When they got to the bottom of the path up the cliff, Sir turned around and said sternly: "Now watch where you're going today. Please don't run into me. Being run into is very bad for the nerves."

Elliott nodded and Sir started climbing slowly up the path. Elliott kept a good distance between them, so that if he tripped or lurched he would not run into Sir. It was hot work. The path was steep and dusty. But they kept winding upward and in no time at all they reached the clearing on the cliff. Oh, the trampoline looked simply grand. Quite large. And very sturdy. By the time they had finished last night, they couldn't really see what it looked like. But now . . . it was simply splendid. "Sir, doesn't it look grand?"

"Indeed it does, indeed it does, my boy. Simply grand. But let's get to work. Give me the food, you go get the suspenders and the hammer and nails. We can accomplish quite a lot if we work quickly."

Elliott was very excited. "All right, Sir. Here's the food." Elliott ran over to the rabbit hole and dragged out the suspenders and the hammer and nails. They were a little damp, from last night's dew, but otherwise all right. He took them over to the trampoline frame where Sir was pacing about. Sir spoke: "Now the first thing we'll do is lay out the suspenders on the ground, inside the frame. Let's see. How did we figure it?"

"I know, Sir. We decided to have 54 pairs of suspenders going across and four pairs of suspenders going lengthwise."

"No, boy. That doesn't work out. I remember vividly that we collected 62 pairs of suspenders. That must mean . . . hmmmm. What DOES that mean? I wish we'd written it all down when we figured it out."

"Well, actually, Sir, it doesn't make any difference what we figured out. We HAVE 62 pairs of suspenders. That's 104 single suspenders. And . . ."

"And WHAT? It's a knotty problem, that's what!"

"But, Sir . . ."

"Be quiet, boy. Let me think. You say that we planned on having 54 pairs of suspenders going across. That's 108 single suspenders. That leaves . . . hmmmmmmm . . . 62 minus 54 . . . leaves . . . leaves . . . hmmmmmm . . . that's a hard one. I hate to subtract bigger numbers from smaller ones in the first row. I mean, you know that the bottom number is smaller than the top number, but when you start, it looks bigger. Wish I had some paper. 62

minus 54 leaves . . . EIGHT. It leaves EIGHT, boy. How's that for lightning arithmetic?"

Elliott wasn't particularly impressed with the lightning part, but he hadn't been able to figure it out at all, so he was impressed with Sir.

Sir went on: "So, my dear boy, we have 52 pairs going across and eight pairs going lengthwise. But since the trampoline is almost twice as long as it is wide, we'll have to use two suspenders attached together somehow to make one length. And that means, in terms of single suspenders, that we'll have 108 going across and eight going lengthwise. That should make a very sturdy mat."

Elliott felt quite dizzy and longed to take a little nap. But he tried to look smart and said: "Yes, indeed, Sir. My, you are clever."

"It's all paying attention, boy. All you have to do is pay attention and you can solve nearly any problem. And we have two problems right now. First, how to construct the mat and, secondly, how to attach two suspenders together to make the lengthwise pieces. They are equally important, but we shall take the first one first."

Elliott was very glad that, in the beginning, he had had the good sense to enlist Sir Augustus in this project.

Sir steamed onward. "Now, boy, take note. The natural shape of a suspender is an X . . . a big X. Therefore, we must USE that shape to make the mat stronger. Now, tell me, how can we do that, boy?" He looked Elliott in the eye and waited impatiently.

Elliott rolled his eyes. "Sir, I really don't know. I'm downright dizzy with confusion..." Sir looked very, very stern. Elliott stammered, "I don't know, Sir. I really don't know." He felt very foolish.

"Don't know what they teach you in school. Don't know why you go to school. Logic, boy, logic. THINK."

"Sir, PLEASE tell me. I really can't think."

"All right. I'll tell you. But when we are done with all this silly business . . . when you can do your flip . . . then . . . then I'm going to give you a course in logic. A COMPLETE course."

Elliott didn't like the sound of that. It sounded exceedingly dull and it sounded like hard work, too. "Sir, please tell me how."

"All right. I'll tell you. Actually, it's quite simple. We simply overlap the X's." He stared sternly at Elliott.

Elliott felt dizzy again. "Overlap the X's?"

"Yes. We overlap the X's. Do you understand?"

"No, Sir. I'm sorry. I don't understand at all."

Sir looked suddenly quite fierce. "Come here, boy. I'll show you. It's very simple." Sir Augustus deftly plucked one suspender from the tangle and straightened it out. Then he picked up the hammer and some nails. Then he placed two of the suspender ends on one side of the trampoline frame. Then he nailed them firmly down. Then he took the other two ends and nailed them firmly down to the other side of the trampoline. Then he took another suspender and . . . indeed . . . overlapped the X's. He nailed one end of the second suspender between the ends of the first suspender. Then he did the same thing on the other side. After he finished, he looked up impatiently at Elliott and said, "See, boy. See. Overlapping the X's. It makes a stronger mat that way. Do you think you understand now?"

Elliott did understand. "Yes, Sir. Of course. It's so simple. All that arithmetic must have tired my brain. Of course. It's a splendid idea. Simply splendid."

"Well, do you think you can do it? I feel quite tired. I'd like to sit in the shade for a few minutes."

"Oh, of course, Sir. Of course. I'll do the rest of it right now. You rest for a while."

Elliott felt very optimistic and clearheaded all of a sudden. Sir went and sat down under a tall, kindly tree and Elliott, counting VERY carefully, overlapped the suspender X's all the way down the sides of the trampoline frame. Occasionally, he would stop to count the suspenders and measure the frame. But the work was easy and went quickly. In what seemed no time at all to Elliott, he had overlapped 108 suspenders and nailed them to the sides of the frame.

Sir appeared to be quite sound asleep, but Elliott couldn't wait for him to wake up. The trampoline was ALMOST finished. He ran over and tugged at his shoulder. "Sir. Sir. I've nailed on all the suspenders. What now, Sir? What now?"

Sir woke up and shook his head. He got slowly to his feet and walked over to the trampoline. "Yes, boy, you got the idea. It's a good job. A very good job. Now all we have to do is figure out how to attach two suspenders to

each other and then weave the double length through these."

Elliott said: "Maybe we could tie them together."

Sir said: "No. That won't do. One bounce and the knots would come unknotted."

"But, Sir, I've heard of some very, very strong knots."

"Do you know how to tie them?"

"Well, no." Elliott felt quite silly.

"Well, boy, then there's no point in talking about them, is there?"

"I guess not, Sir. But I have read about sailors making knots that never come undone. No matter what happens, they don't come undone."

"But, boy, *we* don't know how to tie those knots. Besides, tying rope is probably easier than tying suspenders."

"Yes, Sir." He thought as hard as he could, but he couldn't think of a way to attach the suspenders to each other.

stapling machine. Now put the flat rock on the ground and that will be our surface. See!" Sir was very pleased with himself and Elliott thought he should be. It was all very clever, though he still wasn't awfully happy about jumping up and down on nails.

"Now, boy, you bring the suspenders over and place them on the flat rock and I'll give them a sharp rap with this heavy, round stone and they'll be stapled. Just like that!"

Elliott brought the first suspender ends to Sir and put them on the rock and Sir gave them a sharp rap. They looked anxiously at the result. It WORKED! The two ends of the nail had flattened out just like a staple. It looked very strong. "Sir, maybe we should test it . . . by pulling or something."

"Good idea, boy. Good idea. You hold on to one end. I'll hold the other. You pull as hard as you can." Sir and Elliott, holding onto the ends of the suspenders, backed away from each other and Elliott pulled as hard as he could. Harder. Harder. He was pulling very hard. Nothing happened.

"Stop pulling now, boy. Let's look and see if we did any damage."

They moved together and looked at the "staple." It was still as tight as ever. "It works, boy! It works. A splendid idea, if I do say so myself. And see how flat it is. You won't even know the nails are there when you're bouncing up and down."

Elliott nodded. It certainly looked all right. In no time at all, they had fastened the rest of the suspender ends together. Each time Sir gave a sharp rap to one of the U-shaped nails, Elliott held his breath. But it worked every time.

When they had finished fastening the suspenders together, they wove the double lengths through the suspenders on the trampoline frame and nailed the ends down.

There it was! Elliott's trampoline! It looked

very solid. It was beautiful. Elliott thought it was the most beautiful thing he had ever seen.

Sir said proudly: "There it is, boy! Isn't it beautiful?"

"Oh, yes, Sir. It's beautiful. BEAUTIFUL!"

"All right, boy. Climb up on it. Be quick. Test it out. Joggle about. Test it, boy. Quick!"

As he walked over to the trampoline, Elliott felt nervous and scared and silly and brave and proud all at once. He leaned on the trampoline.

"Go on, boy. Go on, get on with it. Climb up and see how it is."

Elliott slowly climbed onto the trampoline. Since he had never been on a trampoline before, he had no real idea of what a trampoline should feel like. He thought it didn't really matter whether it was a good trampoline, compared to other trampolines. All that mattered was whether he could bounce on it and bounce high enough to do a flip. Oh, he loved this trampoline, without even trying it.

He clambered into the center of the mat. It was quite joggly. The feeling was a silly one. It was the silliest feeling he'd ever had. He giggled.

Sir said sternly: "No laughing allowed, boy. This is no time for silliness and giggles. Now stand up and do whatever one does on a trampoline. No nonsense, boy."

Slowly, Elliott stood up. He was suddenly taller than Sir, but he was bouncing. He was bouncing up and down without moving. Just gently bouncing up and down. It was impossible for him to stand still. He wiggled a little and bounced harder. He tried very hard not to giggle, but he couldn't control himself.

"Elliott . . ."

"Sir, I can't help it. It feels so silly. It just makes you giggle. I'm standing still, but I'm bouncing."

"Well, jump, boy. JUMP!"

Elliott essayed a little jump. And suddenly

he was bouncing high. Up and down. Up and down. Up and down. It was wonderful. He couldn't stop. It was wonderful!

Elliott had actually forgotten that Sir was watching him until Sir said: "My, that looks like lots of fun. How does it feel?"

"It feels like lots of fun, too. It's wonderful, Sir!"

"Do you think it's a good trampoline?"

"I think it's a WONDERFUL trampoline. I think it's the best trampoline in the world." All the while Elliott was talking, he was bouncing up and down and his voice vibrated as if he were slapping himself on the chest while he talked. It sounded very funny . . . not like his regular voice at all.

"Boy, will you stop bouncing for a minute? You're giving me a headache. Besides, I want to talk about our plans and I can't concentrate with you bouncing around like a rubber ball up there. Stop now!"

It suddenly occurred to Elliott that he didn't

know how to stop. When you jumped up and down on the ground, you just stopped and that was that. But on the trampoline, you stopped, but you didn't stop. You went right on bouncing up and down. Elliott decided that if he made his body very stiff, he would stop. Stiff things don't bounce. So he made himself very stiff and promptly fell over backwards.

It didn't hurt, but it certainly surprised him. He untangled himself and tried to get up, but it was very hard. There was nothing solid to push on. He finally crawled unsteadily . . . bouncing slightly all the while . . . over to the edge, and looked at Sir.

"Well, how do you like it, boy?"

"Oh, I love it, Sir. I love it. And I want to thank you. I couldn't have done any of this without you. Oh, Sir, thank you so much for all your help and your good ideas. THANK YOU. Maybe someday I can do something for you. Something grand!"

"Don't thank me yet, boy. The most important work is yet to come. You have to learn how to flip now. After all, that's the point of all this. The flip probably won't take as long as making the belts and trading them for suspenders and building the trampoline, but it's the most important work. It's the reason for everything else. Now let's have something to eat and then you can start working."

Elliott felt very happy and peaceful. Now that he had a trampoline and had bounced on it, he felt very close to his dream. He knew a flip wasn't easy . . . especially for an elephant . . . even the smallest elephant of all . . . but he somehow felt that he could do it.

Sir and Elliott sat under a tree and had some tea and grapes and ivy leaves. Sir said: "My, I hadn't realized how tired I was until we sat down. Are you tired, boy?"

"A little bit. But I'm too excited to be really tired."

After they finished eating, Sir suggested

that they sit and rest for a few minutes . . .
to let their food digest. But Elliott said:
"No, Sir. You rest. But I'm going back to
the trampoline. The sooner I can do my flip
the better. Shall we sell tickets to the event?"

"No, boy. I think we'll have a picnic up here
for all the elephants in our part of the forest
and then you can do your flip. My, my! Won't
they be surprised. Why, they may make you
president of the forest."

Elliott blushed: "Oh, no, Sir. I don't think
so. An elephant doing a flip is a grand thing,
but it isn't THAT grand! I'm going to start
practicing now. Why don't you watch from
here? It's such a nice, cool spot."

"All right, boy. Do well and don't work
too hard."

Elliott ran over to the trampoline and
climbed on. He felt a little surer of himself
this time and bounced to the center of the mat.
While Sir dozed in the shade, Elliott bounced
on the trampoline. He quickly learned that

the point of a trampoline is that it helps you to do things which would otherwise be quite hard, if not impossible. It makes all of your movements easier.

For a while, he bounced up and down in one place, going higher and higher. He learned that he could slow himself down by slightly, ever so slightly, stiffening his knees. Then he jumped forward and backward and from side to side. He was concentrating so hard that he didn't even think about giggling. He didn't think about time either.

Suddenly, he noticed that Sir was standing quite close and watching him. He said: "Elliott, do you realize that you've been practicing for three hours. It's almost sundown. I think that's enough for today. Come now, get down and let's go home."

Elliott really didn't want to stop at all, but he knew Sir was right and he suddenly felt terribly tired. He stiffened his knees ever so slightly, stopped bouncing and walked over

113

to the edge of the trampoline and jumped down. His legs felt like rubber. He had been bouncing for so long that he could hardly walk at all. In fact, he felt very wobbly. "Sir, I've forgotten how to walk!"

"Relax, boy. Stand still for a minute. It'll come back to you."

In a few minutes, Elliott was used to being on solid ground again. As they went down the path, the sun dropped into the far mountains.

Sir said: "Why don't you come to my house for supper, boy? You're probably much too tired to cook. We'll have a little celebration in honor of the trampoline."

"Oh, Sir, that's a wonderful idea."

So they went to Sir's house and had some delicious grass cakes and fricasseed palm fronds and cold grape juice and after Elliott helped Sir wash the dishes, he went home to bed and slept very, very soundly.

For the next three days, Elliott and Sir

climbed up to the trampoline early in the morning and Elliott practiced all day long. In the beginning, his leg muscles hurt a lot, but Sir told him that if he kept practicing, they would stop hurting. They did.

Elliott practiced all sorts of tricks . . . turning around in the air . . . bouncing from his feet to his knees and back to his feet . . . bouncing on one foot . . . sitting down and standing up, while bouncing. Sir said that his progress was astounding.

That pleased Elliott very much. Each night when he went to bed, he would whisper to himself, "My progress is astounding," and go off to sleep to dream of astounding feats on the trampoline.

On the morning of the fourth day, as Sir and Elliott were walking up the path, Elliott decided to try the flip after lunch. In case he might want to change his mind later, he didn't tell Sir. Besides, it was nice having a secret.

All that morning, while Sir watched, Elliott

practiced bouncing . . . higher and higher and higher . . . all over the mat. By lunchtime, he could bounce higher than Sir's head, which was very, very high, because Sir was a large elephant. It was terribly exciting.

After lunch, Sir went, as was his habit, to take a nap in the shade and Elliott went back to the trampoline. He felt a little scared and nervous. He thought that it might be bad luck to do it when Sir wasn't watching, because Sir had been with him from the start. But, at the same time, he decided he'd rather try the first flip with no one watching. It wouldn't be so embarrassing if he couldn't do it.

Elliott climbed up on the trampoline and walked slowly to the center of the mat. He began to bounce . . . higher and higher and higher. He felt very frightened. He bounced higher . . . higher than he had ever bounced before. He bounced for a long time and suddenly he gave a mighty pull and twist to his legs and over he rolled . . . way up in the air

. . . it seemed ever so slow . . . down and down he dropped . . . and he landed on his feet.

HE'D DONE IT! HE'D DONE A FLIP! It didn't matter if no one had seen him do it. Elliott, the smallest elephant of all, had done a flip! He was the first elephant in the world to do a flip. He did it on a cliff above the forest, with no one watching but the sun and the clouds. It was the finest moment of his life.

Elliott clambered down off the trampoline, tears streaming down his cheeks, a big smile on his face, and ran over to Sir. He shook him awake and shouted: "I DID IT! I DID IT!"

Sir looked very confused. "What, boy? What?"

"I DID A FLIP!"